Cotton Mill ·Town·

by Kathleen Hershey

illustrated by
Jeanette Winter

Dutton Children's Books
New York

Lovingly dedicated to my grandmother,
Della Faircloth Deaver,
and to my aunt and uncle,
Essie and Sam Ray.

K.H.

Text copyright © 1993 by Kathleen Hershey
Illustrations copyright © 1993 by Jeanette Winter
All rights reserved.
Published in the United States 1993 by
Dutton Children's Books,
a division of Penguin Books USA Inc.
375 Hudson Street, New York, New York 10014

Library of Congress Cataloging-in-Publication Data

Hershey, Kathleen.
Cotton mill town/by Kathleen Hershey;
illustrated by Jeanette Winter. — 1st ed.
p. cm.
Summary: A visit to Grandmama provides lyrical moments
of peace and pleasure, picking huckleberries or
catching tadpoles in the goldfish pond.
ISBN 0-525-44966-3
[1. Nature—Fiction. 2. Grandmothers—Fiction.]
I. Winter, Jeanette, ill. II. Title.
PZ7.H432426Co 1993 92-7379
[E]—dc20 CIP AC

Designed by Sara Reynolds
Printed in Hong Kong
First Edition
1 3 5 7 9 10 8 6 4 2

I wish I lived in this cotton mill town where my grand-mama lives.

Here the cotton flowers turn from white to pink on bushes planted in long, straight rows. There is a mill pond which is still and quiet until it spills over the cement wall.

Aunt takes me swimming there when she gets home from work at the drugstore. It's fun to swim until the sunset turns the water gold.

I wish I lived in this cotton mill town where the woods are close and dark, and tiny animals peep out at me with shiny eyes, and rabbits bounce by so fast I barely see them.

I can pick violets for Grandmama's table and pull the thread from the wild honeysuckle blossoms to taste with my tongue.

I wish I lived in this cotton mill town where huckleberries
grow dusty blue by Mud Cut Creek. They stain my mouth
and fingers when Grandmama takes me berrying.

Grandmama wears Uncle's trousers for berrying. When we wade through Mud Cut Creek, she goes first, with the legs rolled up and over her knees.

The blue stains stay on my fingers even after I catch tad-poles in Aunt's goldfish pond.

The tadpoles hide under the flat water-lily pads, but I catch six in my jar.

I wish I lived in this cotton mill town where Grandmama grows field peas, okra, cabbage, butter beans, and corn.

She has two long rows of pink gladiolas to make bouquets for the church.

The dirt is black and full of earthworms.

Grandmama fills a can with dirt and worms for times when
we go fishing.

I wish I lived in this cotton mill town where the nights are cozy.

Missy the cat curls up with her kittens, and Uncle beats
all of us at Chinese checkers.

Grandmama winds the clock on the mantel every night
before she goes to bed. Granddaddy's picture is on the
mantel too.

When Granddaddy was alive, he worked in the cotton mill. He wore bib overalls and round-toed boots that laced all the way up his ankles.

I wish I lived in this cotton mill town where the hammock hangs under the sweet gum trees. I can read all day if I want to—except on the days when we go fishing.

Then Grandmama wakes me so early it's still dark outside.
She's wearing Uncle's trousers again.

We two walk the railroad tracks and over the trestle and down a hill. The sun climbs to the top of the pine trees and lights the water that travels from the mill pond to rest here.

Grandmama catches a mess of fish. She never tells anybody
I only caught a stick.

I wish I lived in this cotton mill town where sometimes
Grandmama and I go to work at the peach farm.

We ride with our friends in the back of a truck all the way
to the packinghouse.

The kids stand and watch peaches move on rollers. Our job is to pull out the culls. The culls are the sweetest and best, but they'll spoil before they get to the city.

I eat too many.

I wish I lived in this cotton mill town where Grandmama buys me ice cream when we walk to the post office to get the mail.

Grandmama's box is number 584. My letter is from Mama. It says she and Daddy miss me.

My mama knows that sometimes I wish I lived in this cotton mill town where she grew up. But I have to go back to the city now.

Mama says I can choose one of Missy's kittens to take with
me. I chose the white kitten. I'm going to name it Cotton.